SOCIAL ENGINEER

Ian Sutherland

ISBN: 0-9930056-1-6
ISBN-13: 978-0-9930056-1-9

For Laura and Raquel, who constantly remind me through their own actions that in order to live your dreams you must be dedicated and apply yourself. Always.

CHAPTER ONE

Six Days Ago

Dr Robert Moorcroft entered his office in the North Wing of HTL's head office campus. He hung up his white lab coat behind the door and poured himself syrupy coffee from the glass flask. While he had been in the meeting reviewing the latest results of the pharmaceutical company's new Alzheimer's drug, the ochre liquid had stewed on the percolator machine's heating element for most of the morning. He decided it should still be passable.

His mobile phone bleated from the holster on his belt. Unhooking it, he noticed the display showed a mobile number, but not one stored against a contact in the phone.

Immediately thoughts that Madeline, his beautiful wife of eighteen years, had been involved in another car crash raced through his mind. She'd had three in the last four months, but none had been serious. While she hadn't yet been formally diagnosed, he was intimately familiar with the early signs of dementia, and suspected he should talk her into scheduling a check-up at the local GP surgery. He was dreading facing her initial reaction and the inevitable changes it would cause to their lifestyle, when, no doubt, the diagnosis would be confirmed.

"Hello?" he said into the phone.

"Dr Moorcroft?" The deep male voice sounded serious.

"Yes, who's this?" And, before he could help himself, "Is Madeline all right?"

"Madeline? No, I'm not calling about your wife, Dr Moorcroft."

"Who is this?" And, more importantly, how did whoever it was know Madeline was his wife?

"I'm not at liberty to say. You may call me Mr Smith for the sake of expedience."

"I'm putting this phone down unless you immediately explain yourself, *Mr Smith*."

"I work for GCHQ in Cheltenham. Does that name mean anything to you?"

"Yes, but only from the news. Something to do with government spying. MI5 or MI6."

"Yes, that's us. Among other things, we're the agency responsible for providing intelligence analysis based on electronic communications to the other government departments."

"Okay. But why the hell are you calling me?" And, although Moorcroft didn't give voice to the thought, why call him on his mobile?

"One of our responsibilities is to protect British economic interests. As part of this remit, we've built up a liaison service with many of the larger UK headquartered multinational organisations."

"Yes?"

"Let me cut to the chase. Does *Project Myosotis* mean anything to you, Dr Moorcroft?"

It meant a lot. It was HTL's internal codename for their major

Alzheimer's prevention drug research program; Myosotis being the Greek name for the flowers more commonly known as forget-me-nots. It was the research project the whole company's future was staked upon. Project Myosotis was about two years away from clinical trials, but initial results were incredibly promising. Moorcroft's unspoken hope was that, by the time clinical trials were in play, Madeline's dementia might become a treatable case.

"Maybe," he said cautiously. "But how do you know this name? It's not in the public domain."

"As part of our electronic surveillance program, we've been intercepting some traffic relating to Chinese hacker groups. They may be working for large Chinese corporations or could even be state sponsored; it's hard to tell. It seems that they've been targeting IP addresses registered to HTL, Dr Moorcroft. We believe they are attempting to infiltrate your company's security defences and steal your secrets. I'm calling you now to bring this to your attention so that you can defend yourself appropriately. As I said, it's not in Britain's best economic interests for our country's intellectual property to be stolen by the Chinese."

"Are you sure HTL is being attacked?"

"Dr Moorcroft, we uncovered the term Project Myosotis from these intercepts. It seems to mean something to you, so I'd suggest that they're making some progress."

"But that's impossible. Our Security and IT departments assure me that we have implemented the very best cyber defences."

There was silence on the other end of the line. Moorcroft slowly digested the implications.

Smith attempted to placate him. "Even the best defences can still be compromised, Dr Moorcroft. It may be that the hackers have only gained peripheral access. I'm sure your firewalls and intrusion detection systems would have notified you of any unusual activity."

"Yes, I'll check with IT."

"Good. And you could also . . ."

"What?"

"Well, I was going to suggest that you have a penetration test performed, but I'm sure your IT department has those done regularly."

"Penetration test?"

"Hiring someone to test your cyber defences, as if they were a hacker attempting to break into your systems. It's the best way to know for sure if you have any weaknesses. If they find anything, they'll report it to you and you can put new defences in place."

"I've not heard of our IT department doing that, but then I'm not close to their day-to-day activities."

"Well, there's pentesting and then there's *pentesting*."

"What do you mean?"

"Given the nature of your business, your company lives and dies by its patents and other intellectual property, yes?"

"Yes."

"Well, then maybe you should retain the services of one of the best penetration testers in the industry. They're not all the same, you know. And, if you do it without anyone knowing — especially IT — then it would be a *true* test. A bit like when you do a fire drill. You don't warn employees it's coming, otherwise it makes a mockery of the test itself."

"I see. That makes sense."

"It's like turkeys voting for Christmas. The last thing most Security or IT departments want is to be embarrassed by poor pentest results, so they don't necessarily do it justice. They just hire large IT security companies to make it look like they're doing the right thing. But it's a skilled job and it always comes down to the individuals doing the test."

"Hmmm."

Smith had a point. But the most important point was that GCHQ had intercepted the term Project Myosotis from the Chinese. This was serious. As Head of R&D, Moorcroft had every right to protect the company's interests. No, more than that, as a registered company director, he had a responsibility to protect the company.

It had nothing to do with Madeline's condition, he told himself.

"Is there anyone GCHQ recommends, Mr Smith?"

"Not officially, but . . ." Smith gave Moorcroft the names and contact details for three independent penetration testers.

"I really appreciate your bringing this issue to my attention, Mr Smith."

"You're welcome. Hopefully, you'll never hear from me again."

Smith ended the call. And only then did Moorcroft remember that Smith had called him on his mobile number. He supposed Smith had done it to prove how resourceful GCHQ was.

Moorcroft took a slurp from his coffee and almost spat the disgusting, lukewarm, bitter liquid out all over his desk.

He picked up his desk phone and dialled the number at the top of the list.

* * *

Today, 8:50am

Avoiding eye contact with the three senior executives sitting confrontationally on the other side of the huge oak meeting table, Brody plugged the projector and audio cables into his top-of-the-line tablet computer. The absence of small talk heightened the sense of tension in the room. Brody thought about saying something, anything really, to break the ice, but then remembered he wasn't here to make friends or seek their approval. He was here to make a point.

Not that Brody had many friends, well not in the real world anyway.

It was early on a rainy Monday morning in HTL's head office campus near Shoreham in Kent. The pharmaceutical company's Research and Development Director, Dr Moorcroft, had yet to arrive. Moorcroft had scheduled this meeting immediately following his reading of Brody's report on Saturday morning, which Brody had submitted only the evening before. This had rankled Brody because he'd had to cancel his weekend's plans at short notice, instead using the time to prepare the presentation he was now about to give. And he'd had to set his alarm for some ungodly hour this morning to make it here on time from his apartment in London. He made a mental note to never again submit a findings report on a Friday evening.

A mirror image of Brody's tablet computer materialised on the large screen at the foot of the table. Satisfied the projector worked, he turned the mirroring off. On the desk next to his tablet, his smartphone flashed the receipt of a text message. He picked it up and saw it was from his girlfriend, Mel, confirming she could meet him for lunch later on. He patted his pocket nervously, feeling the shape of the small item it contained.

With nothing left to do but wait for Dr Moorcroft, Brody studied the HTL executives sat silently across the table: two men flanking one woman. Moorcroft had explained during their phone call on Saturday morning that he would summon the heads of IT, Human Resources and Security to Brody's presentation. Moorcroft had not provided names but this hadn't deterred Brody from checking out who they were ahead of the meeting.

He already knew which of them was the Head of Security, having previously researched him as part of the original brief. For the other two, he had browsed through the HTL corporate website and then searched LinkedIn, the 'business' version of the social networking site Facebook, to determine who they were and check out their backgrounds. Based on the photos in their publicly viewable LinkedIn profiles, he was pleased to see his quick investigation had narrowed down to the correct people.

The IT Director was called Rob Hall. His LinkedIn picture presented a lean, tanned face with a full head of hair but the photo must have been taken some years before. In real life, Hall was flabby and overweight with an aggressively receding hairline. He wore an ill-fitting light grey suit with open-necked pink shirt and was intently thumbing through messages on his BlackBerry.

The woman was much younger than her two colleagues, who both looked to be in their mid-forties. She was perhaps in her early thirties, similar in age to Brody. Brody had discovered that she was called Kate Wilson and ran Human Resources. She shuffled some papers and peered at Brody over the top of her rimless glasses, stage-managed to give her the air of seniority denied by her relative youth.

The last was Paul Jacobsen, HTL's Head of Security. According to LinkedIn, he had originally been in the Navy, having served in the Falklands and then, up until a few years ago, had been a senior ranked detective in Greater Manchester Police. He was thin and well groomed, wearing a dark, pinstriped suit, plain white shirt with an inoffensive tie and cufflinks. The job title alone had made Brody believe that the Head of Security would be his biggest obstacle this morning and, watching Jacobsen nonchalantly twirl an expensive Montblanc pen around in his fingers, the impression was reinforced. In fact, having spotted Jacobsen's shiny tan brogues as he entered the meeting room a few minutes earlier, Brody was now one hundred per cent positive there would soon be a head-on confrontation.

Finally, the door opened and Dr Moorcroft entered, wearing a white lab coat over a grey shirt and tie. He shook hands with Brody and, instead of taking the impartial seat at the head of the table, sat in the vacant chair beside Brody and next to the projector screen at the foot of the table.

That evened things up nicely.

Moorcroft asked the HTL executives to introduce themselves. They each provided their names and titles, nothing more. Before Brody could reciprocate, Moorcroft jumped in. "This is Brody Taylor, an independent security consultant. He's here to present the findings of a penetration test I commissioned following the recent hacking attacks from China, brought to my personal attention by GCHQ."

Jacobsen's expensive pen clattered on the table. "Hold on a minute, Bob. That's my domain. What gives you the right to —"

Moorcroft held his left hand up to silence Jacobsen.

"What's a penetration test?" asked Wilson, warily.

Hall turned to her and explained, "A pentest is a method of testing our security defences by simulating computer hacking attacks."

"Mr Taylor, please begin your report," commanded Moorcroft.

"Please, call me Brody."

Brody pressed some keys on the detachable keyboard connected wirelessly to his tablet via Bluetooth. An image appeared on the large screen at the foot of the table. It was a very long chemical formula, with lots of C's and H's.

"Do you recognise this?" Brody asked the group.

Hall frowned. Wilson shrugged. Jacobsen spoke for them, "Just because we work here doesn't make us all chemists."

Moorcroft, who had known what was coming from reading Brody's report, maintained his severe gaze on his colleagues and answered Brody's question. "It's the formula for our new Alzheimer's prevention drug. The one that is still in development, two years away from beginning clinical trials. The one on which the future financial success of HTL is riding. Let me put it this way." Moorcroft leaned forward towards his three colleagues, fists clenched, enunciating each word precisely. "If this formula got into the hands of our competitors, especially an unscrupulous Chinese firm, HTL's future would be *wiped out overnight*." He paused, his eyes not leaving those of his three colleagues, and then asked, "Where did you get hold of this, Mr Tay— I mean, Brody?"

"I broke into your IT systems and stole it from you, Dr Moorcroft," said Brody, matter-of-factly.

"That's impossible!" barked Hall, sitting bolt upright in his chair.

"Impossible?" Brody frowned theatrically. "No, not impossible. I'd categorise it as . . . quite difficult."

Hall countered, "But I've installed the most expensive, most sophisticated perimeter defences in the world! They've withstood hundreds of hacking attacks from all over the planet. Anyway, the new product development system this formula is located on is on a network physically ring-fenced from the main corporate network. It really is impossible to get to from the outside."

"Yes, I agree," conceded Brody, "Your firewalls are hardened well. Very few ports are open to the Internet. No obvious vulnerabilities. It passed a standard pentest."

Hall sat back in his chair, seemingly relieved.

"It's your employees that are the problem," Brody continued.

"Are you saying that one of our employees gave you this formula?" It was Wilson. She had removed her glasses. Without them she looked softer, more approachable.

"Yeah, give me his name," said Jacobsen, "I'll have him dealt with."

"No one employee gave it to me," said Brody. "And you're right, Mr Hall, the new product development system is on a separate network only accessible from within this building. Once I figured that out, I simply walked into the secure area, logged into the system, copied it and emailed it to myself."

"That's impossible!" It was Jacobsen, repeating Hall's earlier denial.

"I thought we were done with that," smiled Brody, coolly. "Have you heard of social engineering?"

Silence.

"I'll take that as a no, then. Let me show you."

Brody pressed a key on his laptop. His chemical formula gave way to a slide containing a video he had recorded last week when he had visited HTL's campus the first time. The video began playing, audio emitting from the ceiling speakers. Brody narrated, "This footage was taken last Wednesday. I'm driving a white van towards this building. There's a high-definition pinhole video camera inside the cap I'm wearing. It has a Bluetooth connection to a receiver in my bag which records everything I see."

The video footage panned towards the rear-view mirror and

Brody's reflection was plainly visible. Under a dark grey cap displaying the trusted logo of Cisco, the world's largest networking equipment manufacturer, his thick head of blond hair and neatly trimmed beard could clearly be seen. From the mirror, Brody grinned and winked cheekily for the camera. Although the onscreen reflection displayed utter confidence, Brody easily recalled the butterflies that had hurled themselves around his stomach at the time.

The image returned to the road, skirting the electric fences surrounding the HTL campus. The camera moved about as Brody's head turned to take in the view. Acres of grass lay beyond the fences. In the distance stood the three-story glass enclosed building they were sitting in right now. Onscreen, two of the wings were visible but there were four in total, each protruding from a central hub in the directions of the compass. The building's shape was a play on the green and black plus sign used in HTL's corporate logo, which Brody knew was originally designed to allude to the Red Cross logo, a meretricious way of engendering brand empathy for the global pharmaceutical corporation.

Approaching the security guardhouse, the screen showed twenty or so weary protestors camped outside, sipping steaming beverages from flasks. Their billboards declared that they were angry with HTL for animal rights violations.

"Idiots," Jacobsen commented. "Every day they're there. They drive me nuts."

"In that case," said Brody, "you'll enjoy the next bit."

In the security hut beyond, a guard looked up from his newspaper, observing the van's approach. The hut had two barriers that raised one at a time, trapping visiting vehicles between them to confirm they had appropriate clearance to gain access. The security guard nodded acknowledgement at the approaching Brody.

The van slowed. The clicking noise of the van's direction indicator could be heard. As one, the activists became animated and began shouting. The high-resolution video footage clearly showed two of the hand-painted signs: "Animals have rights" and "HTL kills primates!" A group of protestors ran for the junction's corner in an attempt to block or slow Brody's access.

Instead of slowing, Brody briefly accelerated and their faces gawped in horror at his unanticipated move. Quickly, they dived out of the way — one, dressed in a pig costume, falling on the grass verge. As if synchronised, the security barrier rotated upwards, allowing the van through. The rear-view mirror filled the image onscreen, showing the barrier descend. Behind it protestors shook fists above their heads.

"Nice move," said two voices in unison. One was Jacobsen and the other one was from the laptop. It was the security guard, whose grinning face now filled the screen. The guard continued, "Shame you didn't hit one of them."

Brody's voice, "Next time, I'll take the corner faster."

Eight Weeks Ago

"An animal rights protestor?" Leroy scoffed. "Are you serious?"

Brody considered his best friend's question, ignoring his laughter.

"What's not to like? Look at her. She's gorgeous!" Brody pointed at his computer screen. The dating site profile for Mel Beaufils filled the screen; her photo front and centre. She had wavy blonde hair and large twinkling green eyes set off by raised eyebrows and an effortless smile, suggesting she had a secret to share. Brody had been intrigued from the moment he'd first viewed her picture, just over a week ago. Through the site, he'd contacted her immediately and, after some emails back and forth, he was now just an hour away from their first date.

"She's not bad," commented Leroy, tilting his head to one side. "A bit too womanly for me."

"That's because this is a straight dating site, you fool. Anyway, you've got Danny."

Leroy and Danny had been an item for many years.

"So, who are you going to be tonight? Brody the cinematographer? Brody the stuntman? Brody the circus clown? Obviously not Brody the computer hacker."

"I'm not sure what I registered as on this site. Hold on a sec, let's check my story." Brody clicked on a link that brought up his own profile. "Ah, now I remember. Tonight Leroy, I'm Brody the location scout."

"Not bad. Easy enough to blag, especially with the amount of movies you watch. Plus you can justify being out of the country for months on end."

"And if you look at my profile, being out of the country so much is the reason I claim to be using a dating site. Just looking for some intelligent company for those rare occasions I'm back in the UK."

"So why is this Mel on the dating site?"

"She says she wants to find an escape from the drudgery of her normal life. She's a nurse in an elderly care home. And on top of that she does loads of charity work as well as being an animal rights campaigner."

"And so she's chosen you? A boring white man. Not very exotic."

"What? So I presume your answer to drudgery is to fuck a black guy."

"Once you've gone black, you never go back," trilled Leroy, momentarily putting on his coyest, campest voice and fluttering his eyelashes. Then regular Leroy returned. "Take Danny. He can't get enough of me, even after four years."

Brody shook his head and raised his eyes upwards as if seeking divine intervention.

"Where are you taking her? Bromptons?"

"Of course."

CHAPTER TWO

Today, 9:10am

Brody's voice came from the speakers in the HTL boardroom. "I'm on a call-out for . . . hold on a second . . ." The image showed Brody's hands retrieve a clipboard from the passenger seat. It contained one piece of paper with a name written on it. " . . . Mandy Jones in IT."

The guard in the security gatehouse confirmed the details matched those on his computer screen. "Are you Charles West from Cisco?"

"Charlie, yes," said Brody. "Only my mum calls me Charles."

"Yeah, well my mum calls me selfish and ungrateful, but that's another story."

Brody laughed obligingly.

"Okay, *Charlie* West. You're on the list. Please head for the visitor's car park. I'll let reception know you're on your way."

"How the hell did you get on that list?" demanded Jacobsen.

Brody paused the video.

"I phoned up your IT help desk and asked them what the process was to get someone registered as a visitor. They simply

15

assumed I was an employee and told me about the guest registration web page on your intranet." He paused briefly, sizing up the opposition. "You know, that's the thing about help desk staff. They just want to *help*."

Wilson made some notes. Hall asked, "You said earlier that you couldn't break through our firewalls. So how did you gain access to the intranet? It's only accessible by authorised employees from inside our network."

"I didn't need to. With that knowledge, I then phoned your reception, pretending to be Mandy in IT. I have the audio recording here by the way, but I'd rather not play it now. My high-pitched impression of Mandy is rather embarrassing!" Brody smiled innocently. "Anyway, as Mandy, I told her I'd already left for the day but had just remembered that I had a Cisco engineer arriving the following morning. And the receptionist — I think her name is Yvonne — kindly offered to fill in the guest registration for me."

"So this is social engineering then?" asked Wilson. "Conning people into doing things for you?"

"In a way, yes. I manipulate people into performing actions or divulging confidential information, which gives me the access I need. It's a method your Chinese competitors could easily employ. Or even those animal activists outside — if they put their mind to it. There are measures you can put in place to prevent this, which we'll walk through later."

Eight Weeks Ago

"What is this?" asked Mel suspiciously, as she looked up and down the deserted backstreet, seeing only a long expanse of redbrick wall. Only the large wooden door they stood in front of broke up the monotony of brickwork. There were no windows. In fact, there was nothing to indicate what the outer walls contained.

Brody already loved her French accent; *this* pronounced as *zees*. Her voice was sweet and she radiated continental charm; a natural innocence that he'd never experienced before, especially from anyone he'd met through the dating site.

"It's a surprise," he said.

He rapped on the door and stood back. Mel wrapped her arms around herself, unsure of her situation. And of him.

It was all going to plan.

The door swung inwards, revealing a huge man in a suit, shirt and tie, all in black. An electronic earpiece was wrapped around one ear.

"Welcome to Bromptons," said the bouncer.

"Evening, Gerry," said Brody, stepping over the threshold.

Brody looked back and saw that Mel remained outside. He reached out a hand and smiled. After a moment's hesitation, she took it and allowed herself to be gently drawn inside. She had small soft hands.

Once Gerry closed the door to the street, he opened an internal door. Immediately, the hustle and bustle of a busy bar could be heard; a tenor saxophone playing mellow jazz in the background. They walked through and were greeted by a waitress, who checked Brody's reservation and asked them to follow her. As they walked through the dimly lit bar, past booths and seating areas separated from each other by black net curtains draped from the ceiling high above, Mel took it all in with an expression of childlike wonderment on her face.

"This is amazing," she said, once they were seated opposite

each other in their own private booth. "How do you know it is even 'ere?"

"This place is called Bromptons. It's a speakeasy: a concept originally invented by the Americans during the prohibition era, when they had to hide their bars and alcohol drinking from the authorities. You had to be in the know to find it — usually a back door in a back street, with all the windows at the front blacked out completely to hide what was going on inside."

"Why is it 'ere, now? And in London?"

"Just a fad, I suppose. But it is cool."

Mel agreed.

As Brody had hoped, the idiosyncrasy of Bromptons had worked its magic, allowing them to fall into conversation naturally, suppressing any of the stiltedness that he otherwise found occurred on first dates. A waitress took their drinks order, and they continued chatting.

Initially, Brody steered the conversation around Mel. She answered his questions openly, neither feigning her responses, nor dressing them up. She described her job as a nurse with passion. She truly cared about the well being of her patients. She offered up amusing anecdotes of randy old hospitalised men. She talked about helping the homeless, attending soup kitchens on her days off. She volunteered in a charity shop near where she lived in Chalk Farm.

He marvelled at her. Mel was unlike anyone he'd ever met before. To give that much of oneself to strangers without a private agenda was something so far removed from Brody's psyche that he found himself mesmerised. But the reward seemed to be her zany lust for life. She laughed easily and took pleasure in the simplest of things.

"And you Brody? What is a location scout?"

He shifted in his seat, but the lies came easily enough. He explained how he worked for film production companies, helping them identify places around the world that would serve the aesthetic needs of the films. He attempted to make it sound boring, talking about budgets and logistics, weather conditions and lighting, and obtaining permission from location owners.

"It's how I came across this place," he concluded. "We ended up using it for a scene in the recent *Sweeney* movie."

"The one with Ray Winstone?" At his nod, she continued excitedly, "What is 'e like?"

"No idea. I never got to meet him. Most of the work I do is pre-production. I rarely get involved once filming starts. Unless there's a problem with the location."

"But you must know where and when movies are being filmed in London?"

"Some," he said hesitantly, having no idea about shooting schedules. "Why?"

"Perhaps you could take me to one when they are filming. Maybe we will see a famous Hollywood actor?"

Brody was pleased with himself. Mel was already talking about a future date, even if she didn't realise what her words had implied. He studied her exquisite features across the table and decided that he would very much enjoy seeing her again.

"Okay, I'll check tomorrow with the production companies and see who's filming in town and where."

* * *

Today, 9:14am

Brody resumed playing the video. It cut to him entering the main reception. A young woman sat behind the reception desk, wearing an unflattering female version of the uniform worn by the guard at the gatehouse. Her bright lipstick and long, manicured nails aided her in maintaining some degree of femininity. She greeted him brightly and verified the details displayed on her computer, just as the previous guard had done.

The receptionist phoned through. The camera panned around as Brody scanned the foyer. Floor-to-ceiling barriers blocked further access into the building. They had proximity sensors that opened when an identification pass was waved within range and authorised by the access management system.

"Hi Mandy —"

The video turned sharply. Brody remembered that he had been shocked, thinking that Mandy had somehow answered the receptionist's call.

" — just letting you know that the engineer from Cisco you were expecting has arrived in reception." She terminated the call. It had only been a voicemail.

Brody's voice said, "I'm not surprised Mandy didn't answer. We've just been texting each other and she's in a meeting that's overrunning. She said she might even be another half-hour or so."

"Well, you're welcome to wait," she replied, indicating the round sofas by the window.

"Sure, thanks." The camera turned and stopped at a mirror reflecting Brody head to toe. As well as the cap, he wore an engineer's grey fleece with the Cisco logo prominently embroidered upon it and carried an aluminium case. He patted his stomach, turning back to the receptionist.

"I don't suppose you know if there's somewhere I can get something to eat? It's been a long drive and I missed breakfast."

"Well, the nearest place would be in the village, but that's a good fifteen minutes drive . . ." She looked at the logo on his fleece and, visibly making up her mind, said, "Actually, we have a staff restaurant onsite. I'm not really supposed to let you through unescorted, but —"

"That would be great. Thanks . . ." Brody read the red security id pinned to her jacket. It had the word 'SECURITY' across the top, her picture and name below. ". . . Yvonne. You're doing me a real favour."

"Okay," she nodded. "Before I let you through I need to give you a visitor pass."

Following Yvonne's instructions, Brody removed his cap. The image turned around to show Brody posing for the webcam connected to her computer. Placing the cap back on his head, the camera then showed her insert a white plastic pass with the HTL logo and the word 'VISITOR' into a machine. A few moments later, it spat out the card with his picture and false name neatly printed on it. She placed it inside a plastic holder with a clip and handed it to him. He attached it to his fleece, careful not to cover the Cisco logo.

"Bob, that's against security policy," whined Jacobsen to Moorcroft. "She should never let someone through unescorted, even to the canteen. I'll have her fired."

Brody paused the footage.

Moorcroft replied coldly, "It gets worse. And, if I were you, Paul, I wouldn't jump too quickly to firing *other* people."

Jacobsen narrowed his eyes.

"Look at it from Yvonne's point of view," Brody jumped in.

"I'm on the list of visitors for someone in the IT department. I look like a Cisco engineer. And the canteen is not in a secure area of the building. She made a judgement call. Training can fix that."

Hall, who had been fiddling with his Blackberry, interrupted. "Hold on a second, you asked for Mandy. She works in my department and I know for a fact that she was on holiday last week. She wasn't even in the building."

"Exactly," said Brody. "Go on . . ."

" . . . So you chose her because you knew she wasn't there. But how could you know that? Not my help desk again!"

"No, they would be unlikely to give me personal information like that. It was much simpler. I used LinkedIn to identify people who work in the IT department. Most people use that site very openly when it comes to posting information about their careers and linking to each other. And, guess what? IT professionals are among the most active users on there.

"Then with a list of names and photos, I went to Facebook. That's where it tends to get more personal. Mandy's Timeline clearly stated she's on holiday. From the pictures she's just posted, I'd say she's in the Maldives."

"Good grief," said Wilson.

"The thing is," the pentester continued, "Yvonne on reception has no way of checking, despite the fact you have the most sophisticated access control systems available. That's something else that you can change. Shall we continue?"

Met, as expected, with silence, Brody pressed a key on his laptop. All heads turned towards the screen once more.

Yvonne showed the onscreen Brody how to use the visitor pass to get through the security gates. She followed him through and helpfully pointed him down the only corridor, explaining that the staff restaurant was at the end. Thanking her again, he turned away and walked past a secure door on his right.

Brody arrived at the restaurant double doors, his hand pushing one slightly ajar. He turned his head, the image panning around quickly. Yvonne was still staring at him. Brody waved thanks to her with his other hand. She smiled and turned away, walking back through the barriers.

"Phew, that was close," Brody's voice whispered a note of relief from the speakers, but in real time, he shifted uncomfortably in his seat. He'd forgotten he'd spoken aloud and had missed it when he'd edited the video for this morning's meeting. He wished he'd cut it out.

"If Yvonne hadn't turned around then, I'd have had to enter the restaurant and I'd have lost a good ten minutes going through the motions of buying coffee and drinking it," Brody felt the need to explain.

The onscreen Brody returned to the security doors he'd passed a minute before. The screen jogged momentarily and the audience heard some fumbling noises, and then his hand held up an HTL pass in the name of 'Colin Renshaw' to the camera. It was yellow, with the word 'EMPLOYEE' printed across the top. The picture on this pass showed the grey-haired, clean-shaven and lined face of a much older man, quite different to Brody's youthful appearance. Brody swiped the pass at the proximity sensor and the doors swung open.

Jacobsen leaned forward. Brody paused the playback.

"Oh, for fuck's sake!" said Jacobsen, his teeth bared. "I know for a fact it's impossible to fake those security passes. They have military-grade secure RFID technology embedded in them."

"It's not a fake," said Brody.

* * *

Seven Weeks Ago

Brody waved his pass at the underground station turnstile. The barrier opened and he waltzed through. Behind him, Mel did the same. He held out his hand. She took it and together they ran up the steps to the streets above.

Laughing, they jogged along Tooley Street, which ran parallel to the south bank of the Thames. It was eerily quiet, this early on a Sunday morning. Through gaps between office buildings, Brody occasionally caught sight of boat masts on the Thames and the iconic Tower Bridge. They reached a small side street and turned into it, coming to an abrupt halt when they saw the crowds of people and parked vehicles ahead of them.

Mel squeaked in delight. "Do you think we'll see 'im?"

"According to the filming schedule, they'll be here all day."

She squeezed his hand in anticipation. Together they approached the crowd. Film production crew vans were parked up alongside the road, in front of a tunnel that disappeared under the railway lines above. Film cameras were positioned high on cranes, along with powerful lighting.

As they neared, a barrier blocked further access. A group of fans stood around it, buzzing in anticipation. Brody and Mel joined them, blending in. As if on queue, a door to one of the cast caravans, parked up beyond, opened and a figure descended. The women in the crowd around them began screaming.

Brody observed Mel's jaw drop at the sight of the Hollywood A-lister. He had seen some of the heartthrob's action movies, and hadn't been particularly impressed. The star seemed to always play himself, rather than the character written in the screenplay. Brody thought about some of the social engineering charades he had pulled off over the years and wondered if perhaps he might be the better actor. After all, his performances *had* to work first time; there was certainly no opportunity for a retake.

The leading man waved at the crowd of fans, a huge grin overflowing with white teeth plastered on his made-up face.

"He seems smaller in real life," whispered Mel to Brody, cupping her hand around his ear so that the other onlookers couldn't overhear.

"Yeah, I wonder if he'll film the scene standing on a box so that he's eye-to-eye with the other actors." Having overheard Brody's quip, three of the onlookers turned around and gave him daggers.

Brody held his tongue while they watched the scene being filmed. Finally, after a rather painfully repetitive hour, the director shouted, "Cut!" There was a small ripple of applause. Taking a bow, the actor seemed about to return to his caravan but diverted towards the small group of onlookers when he heard his name shouted by his adoring fans. Smiling genially, he autographed a steady stream of photos and any other memorabilia that they had brought with them. Mel, who hadn't been quite as prepared with the short notice Brody had provided, stuck out her bare arm in the hope the star would sign it. Unperturbed, as if it happened every day, the actor dutifully scribbled his name on her forearm. Mel promised him that she would never wash it again, prompting laughs from everyone in earshot, the actor included. Delighted, Mel grabbed Brody's hand and led him back in the direction they had come, her schoolgirl-like giggles rebounding from the side street around them.

They breakfasted together in Joe's Kitchen and Coffee House, a casual eatery near Borough Station. Brody introduced Mel to the delights of bubble and squeak, which she ordered with poached eggs and hollandaise sauce. To compliment her choice on something so quintessentially English, he ordered a very French Croque Monsieur, topped with a fried egg. They chuckled their way through breakfast, casting doubt on the logic behind their respective countries' cuisines.

Afterwards, they walked along the south side of the embankment, all the way to Westminster Bridge, opposite Big Ben and the Houses of Parliament. It had become a beautiful summer morning. They took selfies with each other on their smartphones, posing alongside human statues. They listened to jazz musicians inside the foyer of the South Bank Centre. They experienced a slow loop of the London Eye, a whole capsule to themselves, admiring the capital's distinctive skyline.

The day passed in a carefree blur.

And later, when Brody walked her to her flat in Chalk Farm, his body tensing in nervousness as he neared her front door, she laughed freely and teased him about his English reservations. She stood on tiptoes and, without hesitation, kissed him, both arms wrapped around his neck. When they pulled apart, she quickly opened the door and pulled him inside.

CHAPTER THREE

Today, 9:22am

Jacobsen was angry. "Are you saying that Colin Renshaw just *gave* you his pass?"

"Kind of," said Brody. "Let me play you this audio."

On his tablet, he opened up an MP3 file with a media player, and the recorded voices from both ends of a telephone conversation could be heard.

"Hello, Colin Renshaw speaking."

"Hi, this is John from HTL Security." It was Brody's voice. "We're just finishing the upgrade for all the ID badges for the new security system at head office. You should have upgraded your pass by now, but my records here say you haven't registered it yet."

"No idea what you're on about, mate."

"Didn't you get the email?"

"No, mate. I get hundreds of emails a day. Must have missed it."

"That's okay, we can sort it out tomorrow when you come into the office."

"Sorry, no can do. I'm off on my hols tomorrow."

"Oh dear. My boss, Jacobsen, will kill me if I don't get them all done by the end of this week . . . Tell you what, I'll arrange for a courier to pick it up from you today. I'll get it upgraded and then I'll leave it with reception for you to pick up when you get back from your holiday. Going anywhere nice?"

Brody stopped the audio. He said, "I picked it up personally that afternoon. The pass is sitting downstairs with reception right now."

Slamming his fist down on the table, Jacobsen shouted, "You used my fucking name in your scam you conniving little —"

"Paul," interrupted Moorcroft sharply, "*enough.*"

Jacobsen stopped himself, but his fists remained clenched around his Montblanc pen as if to crush it.

"LinkedIn and Facebook again, I presume?" asked Wilson.

"Actually, no. I would have used them if there'd been enough R&D personnel listed on LinkedIn, but they don't seem to bother too much with it. I got creative." Brody found it hard to keep the pride from his voice. He pulled up another audio file and pressed play.

"HTL help desk. Can I help you?"

"This is John from the CEO's office." Brody's voice again, but in a confidential manner. "Listen, I need you to keep this to yourself. Mr Musgrave, our CEO, is launching some new employee morale-boosting initiatives. The first one is a chance to win two weeks' hire of an Aston Martin DB9."

"No way!"

"Yes, really. But keep it to yourself. Anyway, to have high impact, we're looking to schedule an all-staff meeting some time over the next week or two. And Mr Musgrave will draw the winner from a hat, live. The car will be presented to the winner there and then, assuming they're on site. And he wants everyone to see it in the car park every day for two weeks!"

"That sounds fantastic."

"Yeah, I know. But here's the problem. We want to make sure that anyone who's on holiday at the time doesn't get drawn. I know it's unfair for them, but it would lose the impact Mr Musgrave wants to have by handing over the keys personally."

"Uh, right?"

"Would you be able to do a search and let me know all employees who've booked annual leave during the next two weeks?"

"Uh, sure."

"You're not on holiday are you? It'd be a shame for you to miss out now you know about it."

Brody stopped the playback. On the other side of the oak table, the executives' jaws had dropped open and they were shaking their heads.

Brody said, "Like I said before, help desks like to help. That's their flaw."

"But he didn't even ask for your employee ID, raise a help desk ticket or anything," stated Hall, the exasperation clear in his voice.

"It's basic psychology. As far as he was concerned I was representing your CEO. And I let him into a secret. He's drawn in and motivated to help."

"Why didn't you just use Colin Renshaw's pass to get through reception?" asked Wilson.

"Good point. It's because receptionists are the people most likely to check the badge of someone they don't recognise. And I look nothing like Colin Renshaw and no amount of make up is going to fix that. You'll see later that no one really checks my badge once I'm through the secure doors. They rely on that having already been done."

Brody brought the video back up. It showed him enter a large atrium open to all three floors. A bank of four glass lift doors lay immediately in front. To the left, a glass staircase offered an alternative to the glass pods that silently glided up and down linking suspended walkways. HTL staff quietly went about their business. A group of three were engaged in conversation on the walkway immediately above. Two women exited a lift and walked towards him. As they approached, they stared directly at the camera.

"They're checking out the Cisco logo on the cap rather than Colin Renshaw's identification pass pinned to my fleece," Brody commented.

On video, Brody made his way up the staircase to the top floor. At the double doors controlling access to the north wing, his yellow pass obligingly turned the light green. He pushed open the doors and strolled along the corridors, passing staff going the other way. No one took any notice of him.

The onscreen Brody made it through another security barrier successfully. Brody remembered thinking at the time that it had almost been too easy.

At another set of security doors, the video showed Brody's hand wave the yellow pass at the sensor. But this time the light above the sensor flashed red. Abruptly, he stepped back from the doors and retraced his steps, the camera pointed at the floor rather than straight ahead.

* * *

Five Weeks Ago

"Brody?"

Brody immediately recognised her voice with its beautiful French accent. Fuck. He couldn't believe his bad luck. What the hell was Mel doing here, of all places?

He turned around slowly, forcing a wide grin across his face. She was sitting in the reception area of the law firm head office he had just been about to social engineer his way into; his latest pentest assignment. Dressed in a navy jumpsuit with a Domino's pizza logo he'd had embroidered onto the chest, he had completed the imposture by carrying in four large flat cardboard boxes containing pizzas. It was a sure-fire way to blag it past any security-conscious receptionist.

He pivoted away from the reception desk — he couldn't continue now — and walked over to the waiting area where Mel was sitting, pulling the boxes up to cover the Domino's logo.

"Well, this is a pleasant coincidence," he said, as amiably as he could make it. She stood as he neared. Leaning forward to give her a kiss, he awkwardly clutched the pizza boxes to his chest. She hesitated, looking him up and down suspiciously, but stood on tiptoes and accepted the peck on her lips.

They had been together for three weeks now and Brody was utterly smitten. Whenever they were apart, his thoughts frequently drifted to her; either reminiscing over their last date or anticipating the next. They saw each other every few days; working around her care home shifts and the weekends she usually spent protesting for animal rights with her activist friends. Occasionally, she stayed over at Brody's apartment and so he had been forced to introduce her to Leroy and his boyfriend Danny. His friends were pleased to see Brody so obviously happy, and particularly delighted that the cause of his happiness was because of someone in the real world rather than the virtual.

Leroy's favourite rant involved Brody's proclivity to prioritise relationships built electronically rather than through interaction with real humans. Brody didn't see the problem, citing Leroy as the exception that disproved the rule. Online, Brody went by the moniker Fingal and had forged friendships and acquaintances with fellow computer hackers from all over the world. He was very active in the hacker forums, always aiming to strengthen his elite hacker status by sharing code, blogging or exposing unknown Advanced Persistent Threats that he'd identified during his pentesting assignments. APTs were crafted by nefarious 'black hat' hackers, often members of mafia-funded cyber-gangs, whose aim was to surreptitiously install them on corporate networks, where they ran undetected, replicating themselves and sending back intellectual property which the hackers could then sell on or ransom. One Russian mafia-backed cyber-gang had even put up a large bounty for any information that led to the unmasking of Fingal in the real world and, for that reason, Brody took extensive efforts to conceal his trail online. Over the years, Brody had worked hard to maintain Fingal's infamy; always ensuring a clear line of delineation between his online and offline worlds.

Spurred on by Mel having met Leroy in his offline world, she had then set up a night out with Joyce, her closest friend in London, and her fiancé Neil. By weekday, Joyce was a lawyer and Neil an accountant. By weekend, both were fellow activists, Mel having first met Joyce three years before at a rally in London. Despite his dismay at being stuck with three activists for the evening, Brody had cheered up the moment Mel had casually introduced him as her boyfriend. It was the first reference to them as an official couple and his mood brightened completely, even outlasting the inevitable boring conversations about drug companies and their immoral use of animals in research.

The only downer was that as their relationship started to become serious, Brody felt ever more guilty about his dishonesty to Mel regarding his online and offline lives. He was stuck in the lie with no obvious way out, reinforcing it that evening whenever Joyce or Neil led the conversation towards him and his background.

"What are you doing 'ere?" Mel asked, suspicion still lining her face. "I thought you were in Brussels, scouting locations."

He thought quickly. "We finished a day earlier than planned. I just got back in on the Eurostar a couple of hours ago. I was going to surprise you later, but obviously that's ruined now." He gave her a sad look and then asked, "What are you doing here?"

"I'm waiting for Joyce to come down. As it is one of my days off, we decided to — how you say — *do* lunch."

"Joyce works here?" Brody couldn't believe the coincidence. Mel had introduced her friend as a lawyer, but it had never occurred to Brody that she would be on the payroll of the exact same law firm on which he was being paid to carry out a pentest.

Mel furrowed her brow. "But what are you doing 'ere, Brody? And what is with the pizzas?"

Brody continued improvising. "I was just getting provisions for the second unit location team. We're in the middle of some long negotiations between our lawyers and the lawyers who represent the owners of Tower Bridge. We want to film an action scene with some boat stunts under the bridge, but they're concerned about potential damage to it from any explosions. I think it's going to be a long day." He shrugged. "Didn't realise our lawyers were from the same firm that Joyce worked for."

Mel studied him, dubiously. "Brody, why are you meeting with lawyers wearing a jumpsuit?"

Yes, that was a good question. Why was he wearing a jumpsuit? The truth was that he was dressed to look like a pizza deliveryman. But he could hardly say that.

"I accidentally spilled a load of coffee over my business suit earlier. This was the only clean thing anyone here could find for me — one of the cleaner's overalls."

She didn't look convinced. He wouldn't have been either. Brody spotted movement in the reflection of the large windows behind Mel. The lift doors were gliding open and Joyce began to walk out. He had to move quickly.

"Damn!" he exclaimed. "I forgot the drinks. Look, I'd better pop back out and get them." He headed for the glass revolving doors that exited back onto the street. "I'll call you later. We'll go out for dinner."

Today, 9:32am

It was time to explain what had happened next to the HTL executives. "So I've reached the limits of Colin Renshaw's access," Brody began. "At this point, I'm aware that an alert has gone off in a security control room somewhere. It's likely they get quite a few each day from real staff inadvertently trying to gain access to the wrong doors. After all, the corridors in this building of yours all look the same to me."

On the screen, he entered a Gents toilet. The video lowered to near ground level as Brody checked the three cubicles for the presence of feet.

The video cut to show a cleaner's cupboard.

Brody had edited out the part of the video where he had stared at his reflection in the large mirror above the sinks, exhaling deeply and telling himself aloud to calm down, the adrenalin causing his hands to shake. If anyone had been in the corridor when he had failed to gain access to that last set of doors, it would have made them instantly more vigilant and very likely caused them to properly check his ID, resulting in a security alert. And, now that he had met Jacobsen in the flesh, Brody doubted that he would have survived such an encounter without it becoming physical. After all, he would have been caught red-handed trying to break into HTL's most secure area. And explaining about a pentest sponsored by Moorcroft would probably have fallen on deaf ears, at least initially.

The cleaner's cupboard had a mechanical combination lock with two vertical rows of seven buttons, labelled with numbers and letters, above a hexagonal handle. That meant many thousands of potential codes. His hand punched in a six-digit code and the door opened.

The off-screen Brody moved his mouse to pull up another audio file.

"Let me guess," said Jacobsen. "You phoned the cleaning contract company we use and pretended to be a new cleaner."

Brody clapped his hands, sardonically. "Well done, you're getting the hang of this." He didn't bother to play the audio file.

The video cut to Brody in front of the mirror. This time he had replaced his Cisco cap with a plain grey one and had donned overalls. He'd located a trolley, carrying a mop and bucket, trays of cleaning materials and a large yellow sack.

He returned to the corridor, pushing the trolley. Slowly, he walked back in the direction of the double doors Colin Renshaw's security pass had failed to open. The nearer he got, the slower he walked. Every couple of yards, the video panned around to check if anyone was coming the other way. But the corridor remained empty.

From the speakers, Brody's voice clearly said, "Bugger," and on the screen, he began to turn the trolley around. At the half-turn mark, the camera moved quickly to show one of the double doors opening. Someone was coming through from the other side. Quickly, he turned the trolley back and rushed the last few yards towards the opening door.

A man in a dark suit was walking through. The camera was pointed downwards, taking in the man's shiny tan brogues as Brody avoided eye contact. In an Eastern European sounding accent, Brody's voice said, "Would you mind?"

A second later the shiny shoes stepped back and the camera nodded thanks, briefly revealing the face of the helpful employee.

In the meeting room, Jacobsen leapt to his feet. "You've got to be fucking *joking*!" Brody flinched as Jacobsen violently flung his expensive pen down on the table but in Brody's general direction. It instantly shattered, three pieces bouncing upwards — one heading straight for Brody's face. Brody reacted quickly and snatched it out of the air. The other two pieces flew either side of him, one just missing Dr Moorcroft.

Onscreen, Jacobsen himself could clearly be seen, obligingly holding the door open. Brody pushed the trolley through. He mumbled an accented "Thank you."

"You're welcome," Jacobsen's voice said from the speakers.

In the meeting room, Jacobsen slumped back in his chair.

CHAPTER FOUR

Three Weeks Ago

Brody held the door open, allowing Mel to pass into the small lobby of the residential block of flats. She pressed the button to call the lift, which opened immediately.

As they rose to the top floor, Brody asked, "Do we really have to do this?"

"Brody, they are my friends. And Neil will be there. You got on well with 'im last time."

Was his acting that good? Neil, Joyce's fiancé, had bored him almost to death the last time they had met. He only had two subjects, both uninteresting: football or animal rights. And worse, tonight Joyce and Neil were hosting a dinner party, with two other activist couples Brody hadn't previously met. He felt like he was walking into a recruitment fair for fresh new protestors. Brody had never given animal cruelty a second thought before meeting Mel, and still couldn't find any reason why he should. Surely, their relationship didn't have to mean they shared each other's hobbies?

The lift door opened and Joyce was there to welcome them

with kisses on both cheeks. She ushered them into her minimalist apartment, all in white except for swashes of colour from large abstract paintings. They were last to arrive. Joyce thrust glasses of Prosecco at them and returned to the kitchen. After shaking hands with Neil, Mel cheerfully introduced him to the other two couples. Brody resolved to stay cheerful and amiably made small talk right up until they made their way over to the large, round glass dining table, where he discovered that the seating arrangement forced each couple to separate. He had been strategically placed between Joyce, whom he knew, and Mary, an American stewardess regularly flying long haul over 'the pond' for US Airways.

He made it through the starter by asking Mary inane questions about her life in the air. He made it through the main course answering questions about his life as a location scout. He used up nearly every anecdote in his carefully researched repertoire, all rehearsed and reused many times, many of which were repurposed from stories he'd originally read in film industry magazines or on Internet gossip sites. At one point, the name-dropping of celebrities made him the focus of the whole table, which he began to find uncomfortable.

As Joyce served dessert and the others compared notes about West End shows they'd seen, Mary unsubtly steered the conversation towards the common interest of the seven companions. She turned to him and asked, completely rhetorically, "Brody, did you know that primates experience pain just as humans do?"

"Do they?" For Mel's sake, he tried to sound interested.

"And did you know how many rhesus monkeys are bread in captivity each year, just to serve the needs of the drug research companies?"

He admitted he didn't know. She told him. It was a high figure. She went on to explain that rhesus monkeys were a particular favourite because the animal is genetically the closest to humans, even having menstrual cycles and similar hormonal patterns.

"And did you know that very few of these animals ever get to see the sun? It's disgusting."

He agreed it was indeed disgusting.

He controlled the urge to ask how else the drug companies might safely test their medicines before human trials began. He knew from skirting around the subject with Mel that it was a pointless question, with the alternatives ranging from testing on human tissue cultures to statistics and computer models. All far inferior approaches.

Instead, he asked her, "Do you think that protesting outside the gates of the pharma companies does much to help?"

"We have to! We can't let them know for a second that we've given up."

"But surely the only thing that would change their practices would be public opinion?"

"Exactly, that's why we do it."

"But, if you don't mind me saying, surely the media needs to cover your protests in order for you to have a chance of influencing the public? Don't you need to be front page material?"

"You're right," Mary admitted. "We're forever trying to find ways to make what we do newsworthy."

"And that's hard?"

"Yes, of course. The cause we're fighting will never be fixed with a single punch. It's a long-term strategy. And the problem with that is that the media always need their interesting sound bite. Something new and tangible."

"Surely there must be an uppercut that would floor the big pharmas?"

"I doubt it. The Holy Grail would be footage from inside one of their research laboratories showing just how badly treated the animals are."

"Makes sense."

"But that's impossible to get. Believe me, we've tried. The resources these companies have at their disposal means that this kind of stuff never leaks. They vet every employee thoroughly. We've tried getting activists on the inside, but never succeeded. Well, once or twice we've got them in but never out with any evidence. Just a verbal account of the cruel things they saw."

"But then it's just your word against theirs."

"Yup." Mary took a large swig of wine and declared loudly: "They're bastards! Rich, inhumane, fucking bastards."

The others halted their conversations at Mary's emotional outburst. And then they all nodded in agreement and began chiming in with similar viewpoints. Brody sat back in his chair, sipping at his wine, and watched them get it all out. Mel threw occasional sympathetic smiles in his direction, understanding that he was enduring the moment on her behalf. Occasionally, he was asked a question and he nodded or shook his head as required. The debate went on for a good twenty minutes, right through coffee, Brody not saying another word, his strategy to avoid upsetting Mel in front of her friends.

It wasn't that Brody's opinion was contrary to theirs. It was just that he didn't really care one way or the other. Huge global corporations got away with murder, literally and metaphorically, all the time. A handful of protestors were hardly going to make a difference. Didn't they realise how the world worked? To him, however noble their efforts, it was a complete waste of time and energy.

Later, as Mel and Brody descended in the lift, she turned towards him and, tiptoeing to reach, planted a big kiss on his lips and then hugged him close.

"*Merci beaucoup*," she whispered.

Relieved to have survived the encounter, Brody hugged her back.

But he vowed never to get himself caught like that again. Nothing was worth suffering that much pointless passion.

"Let's go back to yours," Mel suggested, a seductive twinkle in her eyes.

On the other hand . . .

Today, 9:40am

Brody looked at the contents in his hand. It was the barrel of the pen. He rolled it back across the table towards Jacobsen and goaded the Security Director: "I guess they don't make Montblancs like they used to, eh Paul?"

"Fuck you, Taylor!" the HTL Head of Security snarled in response, but despite the bluster, there was a tone of resignation in his voice.

It was Moorcroft's turn to slam his hand down on the table. "Paul, control yourself. Calm down or leave. Now. Your behaviour is completely unacceptable."

It was unclear whether Moorcroft was referring to what had been shown on the video or his petulant behaviour moments before within the conference room.

At the time, careful not to make too much eye contact, Brody hadn't realised it was the Head of Security himself who had allowed him to tailgate that last set of doors. But when Jacobsen had strode into the meeting room almost an hour earlier, wearing those distinctive tan shoes, Brody had made the connection and realised this presentation was likely to be more fiery than most.

"Is the receptionist still at the top of your firing list?" Wilson piped up. "Eh, Paul?" It occurred to Brody that Wilson didn't like Jacobsen and was taking advantage of this opportunity to twist the knife.

Jacobsen folded his arms in defiance.

Brody looked to Moorcroft for direction. He nodded and so Brody resumed playback. The video footage continued with Brody pushing the trolley. The new corridor had a run of windows on the left-hand side, with views into different laboratories. In the first, white-coated lab technicians worked with different coloured chemical solutions in test tubes and flasks. In another, their colleagues analysed readouts from oscilloscopes, spectrum analysers and other complex electronic equipment. A third showed a bank of cages full of small rhesus monkeys. Brody recalled his conversation with Mary a few weeks before. Seeing the caged animals up close certainly brought to life the monotonous statistics that she had spouted throughout their dessert course.

Brody had edited out the next part of his journey down the corridor. At the time, the ghastly images had made Brody feel faint, forcing him to stop and lean on a pillar to catch his breath. Two gowned lab-workers with masks over their mouths were hunched over a table, their bodies obscuring what they were working on. Next to them, strapped to an operating table, another monkey watched them helplessly, its feverish chattering clearly illustrating its panicked state of mind. When Brody began walking again, his new viewpoint revealed what the monkey on the operating table could see all too well — another monkey lying prostrate on the table, its chest cavity opened up; dead. That time he had turned away quickly, but not before bile rose into his mouth.

The video resumed at a point much further on, through additional security doors that Brody, being on the inside of a secure zone within the HTL campus, only need to press their red exit buttons to pass through. Here, the right-hand side of the corridor was a blank grey wall interspersed with doors. Each door had a window and behind could be seen standard office layouts, with pods containing business attired office workers behind desks and, most importantly, desktop computers.

The screen then showed another pair of men's and women's toilets. The video cut to an image of Brody reflected in the mirror behind the washbasins. He was back in the Cisco engineer's uniform and cap. The aluminium case was open in front of him. His hand retrieved a handful of USB memory sticks and closed the case.

He left a USB stick on top of each toilet roll holder in the three cubicles. Another by the sinks. He braved the ladies' toilet next door and, seeing that one of the cubicles was occupied, just dropped a USB stick by the sink and quietly exited.

Next Brody entered one of the offices. HTL staff sat in cubicles in front of computers or on the phone. Two women stood talking by a water cooler. No one took any notice of him whatsoever. He made his way towards an empty pod near the window, furthest away from the door, and sat down. No one challenged him.

An older man in a shirt and tie sat in the neighbouring pod. He looked up as Brody placed his case on the desk. Brody stole a glance at the Cisco phone handset, rapidly read the digital display and asked the man, "Is this extension two-double-four-nine?"

"Uh, yes it is."

"Excellent. Had a report of some issues with the handset."

Satisfied, the man resumed working. The screen showed Brody opening the aluminium case again. He pulled out a pack of biscuits and an iPhone. The camera then showed him kneel down and climb under the desk. Out of sight, Brody checked for new email messages on his phone. Nothing.

He stood up to find one of the women from the water cooler standing there. In a puzzled voice, she asked what he was doing under her desk. Brody explained that he was the Cisco engineer here to mend her phone. When she pointed out she hadn't realised it was broken, Brody explained the fault was intermittent and reached down, grabbed the biscuits and offered her one. Hesitating at first, she eventually smiled and accepted one. Brody then offered a biscuit to the man in the neighbouring pod, who joked loudly that he'd prefer the phone fault not to be fixed at all, as they could do without any more calls that day. Brody could be heard laughing and promising he'd take his time. The pod's owner offered to go for a coffee to allow Brody more time to work on her phone. Brody offered more biscuits out to other neighbouring pods.

"What's with the biscuits?" asked Wilson.

"Human nature," replied Brody. "When someone is given something, they feel the need to reciprocate. In this case, the owner of the pod gave me time to fix her phone. And the neighbours all bought into it as well."

Onscreen, Brody showed his smartphone to the camera. On the display was a new email. He clicked and it showed a set of usernames and passwords.

"The USB sticks!" exclaimed Hall, as if trying to please a teacher. "You dispersed them in public areas so that it looked like another employee may have dropped it. Someone finds it, inserts it into their PC to see if they can find out who it belongs to."

"You got it. I just put fake files on them, photos mostly. The USB sticks actually have auto running rootkits on them, which start a program called Hacksaw the minute they're inserted. It scans the machine and starts dumping all usernames and passwords to a file and then emails it to me."

The remainder of the video showed Brody logging into the PC on the desk with the credentials supplied in the email. "As you can see, I'm now logged into the network that's physically ring-fenced from the main network. It takes me a while to find my way into the new product development system but, thanks to the biscuits, everyone leaves me to my own devices."

"Brody, I think we've all seen enough," said Moorcroft.

Brody halted the video playback.

Seven Days Ago

Brody felt the need to reciprocate, but couldn't bring himself to say the words, not while he was still trapped within the deception of his own making. He supposed that it wouldn't actually be lying for him to respond with a simple, "I love you too." He really did love Mel and desperately wanted to tell her.

They were lying in her bed; her body spooned into his, both naked and sweaty from their sexual exertions. She had just uttered the words he most wanted to hear. But Mel had declared her love to Brody Taylor, location scout and adopted child of loving foster parents in Jersey, his 'real' parents having died in a car crash with his sister when he was eight years old. But the truth was radically different. His parents were alive and well in nearby Hertford. He had a sister and nephew in Australia. And his profession was 'white hat' computer hacker, hired by large companies to carry out penetration tests.

The silence from his lack of response was as loud as a gong. He hugged her closer and kissed her on the back of her neck. It was the only answer he could give right now.

He felt her tense in his arms. She had expected him to reply with the same endearment. Mel had dared to declare her love first and he had failed to reciprocate.

He resolved to come clean. But the lies of the last six weeks had slowly piled on top of each other, like twigs carefully laid on top of other twigs to make kindling, each supporting the other, but all precariously balanced, ready to light up in flames at any moment.

How could he tell her the truth without hurting her? And risk losing her completely? It was an impossible situation. He should have come clean the morning after they had first made love. But he hadn't. Spinelessly, he had said nothing, allowing the sham to continue.

To fester.

He needed to demonstrate how passionately he loved her. So that, when he finally told her the truth about his life, she would understand and accept, overcoming the treachery of their first six weeks. He knew he couldn't avoid hurting her, but perhaps, if she saw real evidence of the depth of his affection, then maybe their relationship could survive this hurdle.

As she lay in his arms, an idea began to form.

He willed it to gain shape. And, as it crystallised, he realised it might work on more than one level. Not only would it provide the evidence of his devotion and proof of the lengths he would go to in her name, it might also help her see how his craft was ethical. Brody couldn't allow Mel to ever hear the words 'computer hacker' and automatically deduce that he was some kind of cyber-criminal, like the common perception of hackers in the media. He knew her well enough to sense that if she ever formed an impression that what he did for a living was in any way illegal, she would have nothing more to do with him.

The idea became a plan.

The plan became a detailed list of actions in his mind.

He played out the likely scenarios.

And all outcomes led to her accepting the truth. And, once their relationship was on a solid foundation, then he could reciprocate his love for her with complete integrity.

He would execute the plan, beginning tomorrow.

CHAPTER FIVE

Today, 9:55am

Jacobsen had remained stubbornly silent since smashing his pen earlier. Red-faced, he finally erupted.

"This is a fucking joke, Bob! I can't fucking believe you authorised this. You bastard."

"Control yourself, Paul," warned Wilson, her voice a shriek. "We've all got to deal with this."

Brody zoned out of their argument and stopped mirroring his laptop to the large screen.

The raised voices railed on around him, arguing, debating, accusing.

Brody had enjoyed the challenges presented by this pentest, on all levels. He just hoped it would achieve its objectives.

Finally, Moorcroft touched Brody's arm. The arguments had subsided.

Brody looked up. "Sorry, what did you say?"

"I said, Brody, that it's clear that your exploits have shown us exactly how exposed we are."

"True. But most organisations aren't able to defend against an attack of this level of sophistication. However, for every white hat hacker like me, there are plenty of black hats available for hire, every bit as skilled in social engineering techniques."

"He means 'ethical hackers' versus the 'evil hackers' you see in movies," explained Hall, helpfully.

"You've seen what's possible. Unfortunately, there isn't an over-arching patch you can apply for human gullibility but there are some basic protections you can put in place immediately. Most of them revolve around employee education . . ."

Jacobsen remained stubbornly silent throughout the next hour, as Brody led them through a plan of action to strengthen their defences against social engineering based attacks. Hall and Wilson took most of the actions and Moorcroft seemed to relax a little. Ten minutes before the end of the meeting, Jacobsen stood up and left. No one said a word, although Moorcroft raised his eyebrows as if to say, "Well, that's that then."

Brody guessed that was the end of Jacobsen's career at HTL.

Some time later, Brody began the two-hour drive back to London in his metallic orange and black, custom-designed Smart Fortwo coupe. As he drove past the electrified perimeter of the HTL campus, the animal activists, seeing a potential ally in such an in-your-face, anti-corporate, environmentally friendly vehicle let him pass peaceably. He drove slowly, scanning their faces for any he recognised, but didn't spot any of Mel's friends.

If only they realised he'd been the shameless driver of the white van just a few days before.

* * *

Six Days Ago

Brody finished his research and began the hack.

The first step was to call the R&D Director on his mobile phone. Obtaining his private phone number had involved its own convoluted deception. Normally, a search of Companies House would reveal the private contact details, including home address, of all registered company directors, but because this was a pharmaceutical company where directors of such companies had frequently come under personal attack from protestors, new laws had been set up in 2009 to protect their privacy.

In the end, he had phoned the company's switchboard, pretending to be from a printing company with an urgent order for the R&D Director's new set of business cards. It had been his second call to the same number, the first, timed just after midday, had been to make sure that his secretary was out for lunch. Brody explained to the operator that he'd just tried to call the secretary but had only reached her voicemail and that he just needed to confirm the details he'd been provided before he authorised the rush print job; the cards apparently needing to be with their owner by the end of the day in time for a charity function he was attending that evening. Brody read out the details he'd already collected from public sources and then a made-up mobile phone number, which the receptionist dutifully pointed out was wrong and helpfully rectified with the correct number from the employee directory available on her computer screen.

Brody took a deep breath and rang the mobile number.

"Hello?" Male, concern in the voice.

Brody put on a serious inflection, lowering the timbre of his voice. "Dr Moorcroft?"

"Yes, who's this? Is Madeline all right?"

Brody's research had revealed that Moorcroft was referring to his wife; although quite why there was so much concern Brody had no idea.

"Madeline? No, I'm not calling about your wife, Dr Moorcroft."

"Who is this?"

Brody thought about how to respond and decided the more vague and mysterious he sounded, the better his chances. "I'm not at liberty to say. You may call me Mr Smith for the sake of expedience."

"I'm putting this phone down unless you immediately explain yourself, *Mr Smith*."

Okay, maybe a little explanation.

"I work for GCHQ in Cheltenham. Does that acronym mean anything to you?"

"Yes, but only from the news. Something to do with government spying. MI5 or MI6."

"Yes, that's us. Among other things, we're the agency responsible for providing intelligence analysis based on electronic communications to the other government departments."

Brody had lifted that line straight from the Wikipedia entry for GCHQ.

"Okay. But why the hell are you calling me?"

"One of our responsibilities is to protect British economic interests. As part of this remit, we've built up a liaison service with many of the larger UK headquartered multinational organisations."

"Yes?"

"Let me cut to the chase. Does *Project Myosotis* mean anything to you, Dr Moorcroft?"

"Maybe." Brody could hear caution. "But how do you know

this name? It's not in the public domain."

That's where Moorcroft was wrong. A quick search through LinkedIn and Brody had discovered an HTL employee who had specifically listed the name of the project he was working on as part of his publicly accessible résumé. Brody had no idea what the project was about, but a quick scan of the Internet showed him that it was not mentioned anywhere else, meaning referencing it would add credibility to his act.

"As part of our electronic surveillance program, we've been intercepting some traffic relating to Chinese hacker groups. They may be working for large Chinese corporations or could even be state sponsored, it's hard to tell."

Brody enjoyed dropping the Chinese threat into play. Over the last few years, they had become the new bad boys of the Internet, surpassing even the Russians. The US Department of Justice had gone as far as charging members of the Chinese military with cyber-espionage, which Brody found ironic, given the documents leaked by Edward Snowden the year before divulged that the USA had been hacking into Chinese computers for years.

He continued. "It seems that they've been targeting IP addresses registered to HTL, Dr Moorcroft. We believe they are attempting to infiltrate your company's security defences and steal your secrets. I'm calling you now to bring this to your attention so that you can defend yourself appropriately. As I said, its not in Britain's best economic interests for our country's intellectual property to be stolen by the Chinese."

"Are you sure HTL is being attacked?"

Only by me, Brody thought flippantly.

"Dr Moorcroft, we uncovered the term Project Myosotis from these intercepts. It seems to mean something to you, so I'd suggest that they're making some progress."

"But that's impossible. Our IT and Security teams assure me that we have implemented the very best cyber defences."

Brody stayed silent for a few moments, allowing the implications to build. "Even the best defences can still be compromised, Dr Moorcroft." Brody spoke the truth there. "It may be that the hackers have only gained peripheral access. I'm sure your firewalls and intrusion detection systems would have notified you of any unusual activity."

"Yes, I'll check with IT."

"Good. And you could also . . ." Brody deliberately trailed off.

"What?"

It was crunch time.

"Well, I was going to suggest that you have a penetration test performed, but I'm sure your IT department has those done regularly."

"Penetration test?"

Moorcroft was on the hook now. Brody went on to explain what a penetration test was and subtly threw doubt on whether his IT department would hire good enough security testers, not really wanting anyone to show them up publicly.

Eventually, Moorcroft asked, "Is there anyone GCHQ recommends, Mr Smith?"

Brody punched the air in triumph.

"Not officially, but . . ." He proceeded to give him three names, numbers and emails, with Brody Taylor at the top of the list. Whichever choice Moorcroft made, all roads led back to Brody.

Moorcroft thanked him.

"You're welcome. Hopefully, you'll never hear from me again."

Brody, savouring the irony of his closing comment, sat back

and waited for Moorcroft's email to arrive, inviting him to carry out a pentest on HTL.

Now, where would he begin?

Today, 1:10pm

"I have something for you," said Brody.

Mel looked up sharply, her final spoonful of dessert paused on its way to her mouth. She detected the solemn expression on his face and placed it back on the plate, pushing it to one side and giving him her full attention.

He slowly reached into the pockets of his jeans.

A huge beam spread across her face. "You 'ave something for me?" she breathed, reaching out to clasp his other hand across the table.

"I've been wanting to say this since I met you," he said, pulling a small item out of his pocket. "And I thought this would be the best way."

"Brody, it 'as only been two months." She squeezed his hand: a gentle warning. "Please, tell me you're not going to propose marriage."

It took a few moments for him to register what she had just said. He hadn't meant to imply that. What an idiot he was sometimes.

"Marriage? No, of course not . . ."

Her face dropped when he revealed the contents of his hand. He placed the item on the table in between them.

"What is this thing?" Mel asked. Sensing she was in a premonitory moment, she withdrew her hand and wrapped both her arms around herself.

He was relieved she had steered the conversation back on track. "A USB memory stick. But it's what's on it that's important."

Mel inhaled deeply, gathering herself.

"Go on."

"On here is video footage taken from inside HTL's campus in Kent showing intolerable cruelty to rhesus monkeys, all in the name of drug research."

Brody recalled the sickening images and the physical reaction he had experienced at the time. It was one of the sequences he had edited out from his presentation to the HTL executives that morning. At least, he mused, they had got some value from his pentest, even if he had manipulated Dr Moorcroft into hiring him to carry it out in the first place. Once this footage emerged, they would probably link it back to Brody. However, the contact details they had for him were fake. He had made sure they would never be able to track him down again.

Her brows furrowed and she tipped her head to one side, trying to understand.

"It will help you gain new media exposure against the drug companies. I was talking to Mary last week at dinner and she said it's exactly what you all need to ratchet up the campaign to the next level. She said you needed one big uppercut . . . actually I said uppercut, but anyway, one big-hitting punch that the media couldn't ignore." His words jumbled together in his rush to explain. He stopped talking.

Nothing.

He waited a moment before pressing. "I thought you'd be pleased."

"I am," she said. Monotone.

He couldn't help himself, after all the trouble he'd put himself through to get hold of the footage. "You could at least seem so." As the words escaped his lips, he realised how petulant he sounded. The whole idea was for her to be delighted, cushioning the blows from the bombshells yet to come.

"How did you get this, Brody?" she asked, warily.

"Before I answer, I want to step back and explain something."

Mel leaned back in her chair, an obvious gesture to distance herself from whatever was coming.

Brody launched the first barrage.

"Do you remember my advert on the dating site?"

Mel remained impassive.

"Not all of it was true." There, he'd finally said it.

No reaction. He carried on.

"I am not a movie location scout."

She repeated, without intonation. "You are not a movie location scout."

Despite the situation, the film buff in Brody couldn't help recalling the scene in *Star Wars: Episode IV – A New Hope* where, at a security checkpoint, Obi-Wan Kenobi uses the mystical 'Force' to trick some Stormtroopers into believing, "These aren't the droids you're looking for". Fully accepting Kenobi's statement as fact, the Stormtroopers repeat the line verbatim, and allow them to pass unchecked. Brody wished he had The Force at his disposal right now.

He continued, wanting to get it all out. "And I am not adopted. My parents live in Hertfordshire."

Her eyes narrowed.

Brody persevered, more bombs still to drop. "And I have a sister who lives in Australia with her husband. They have an eight-year-old son. My nephew."

Brody stopped and held his breath.

Mel placed her hands in front of her, palms flat to the table and leaned forward.

"You said, 'Not all of it was true.'"

"Yes," he said, hesitating, instinctively knowing she was going somewhere with this but having no idea where. "I did."

"So tell me, Brody. Which part of your story was actually true? Because, from what I can see, *none* of it is true."

She had a point. By way of response, he offered an impotent shrug.

She clenched one hand into a fist and made a soft pounding motion onto the table's surface. Mournfully, she said, "Why, Brody?"

"Because I can't carry on with this stupid deception. And that's because I —"

"— *No*, Brody." She had interrupted, just as he was about to say those three important little words. "Not *why* are you telling me now. I don't care about that. Something like this you should 'ave told me at the beginning. No, I mean, *why* was there a deception at all?"

Oh, that.

"It's because of what I really do for a living."

"What are you?" She laughed, although it was full to the brim with spite. "A porn movie director? A traffic warden?" Her expression hardened. "Please tell me you're not a vivisectionist. I couldn't bear that."

He shook his head and, just as he was about to answer, Mel leapt forward, jolting the table in her eagerness, the wine glasses wobbling before settling still. "You're not embarrassed, are you?"

She placed a hand on his. Was this sympathy? What the hell was going on? Using his free hand, he took a sip of his wine, buying some time.

"Brody," she smiled at him, "I don't care if you deliver pizzas for a living."

Brody choked on his wine. As he coughed and spluttered, she continued.

"I knew it was strange seeing you that time in Joyce's reception carrying those pizza boxes. I told myself there had to be a simple explanation, and not the one you gave me. It makes sense now."

Brody regained his composure. He considered giving up and telling her she was right. It would be so much easier, wouldn't it? Why not continue as they were; just swap one set of lies for another? But, deep down, he knew that was foolhardy.

Slowly, he shook his head. "I wish that was true."

Mel recoiled back to her side of the table. It was time to drop the final bomb.

"I am an independent IT security consultant." He almost wanted to add a "Tah-dah!" Noticing her confused expression, he continued soberly, "More commonly known as a computer hacker."

He allowed the words to sink in.

Suspicion oozed from her voice. "You are a computer hacker?"

"Yes. A white hat, to be specific."

She nonchalantly splayed her palms in front of her to indicate that his last statement had added no clarification at all. The gesture also indicated how seriously pissed off she was.

"Because of the media, everyone believes computer hackers are evil. And yes, there are many that are. They are called *black* hats. And then there are those who do what they do to help companies improve their defences. They are called *white* hats. I am a white hat. Companies pay me to attack them and afterwards I help them fix the holes I discover in their defences, so that they can stop the black hats getting in."

It was just about as simple as he could make it.

"So why?" Her tone was steely.

He wasn't falling for that a second time. "Why what?"

"Why did you make up your profile on the dating site? Why not tell the truth if it is as simple as you say?"

"Because of all the negative connotations associated with being a computer hacker. No one would choose to date one. They would feel unsafe, that their identity was going to be stolen or something worse. And then there's the fact that everyone thinks techies are boring. They think 'nerd'. They think 'geek'. They think 'anorak'. Who's going to want to date someone like that?"

"And the rest of your description? Why not have some truth in it?"

Mel had a point.

As a social engineer, he had become so used to lying about himself that he had never given it a second thought. Also, there was the fact that, under his online persona as Fingal, he was on the wanted list of some of the world's most nefarious cyber-gangs, many of which were backed by the Russian mafia. They would exact a terrible revenge if they somehow tracked Fingal down in the real world. Not only would Brody be at risk, but so would those close to him.

But Brody had already upset Mel enough. He didn't want to add salt to her wounds.

Instead, he played his trump card, hoping it would be enough.

"It is because I am a hacker that I was able to get hold of this," he pointed to the USB stick laying on the table. "I hacked into HTL and obtained this footage. Footage you and your friends can put to good use. Partly, I did it in the vain hope that it might begin to make up for the last two months. But most of all I did it to prove how much I —"

"— *enough*." Mel held up her hand to silence him and hastily stood, her chair toppling backwards. It clattered to the floor, causing other diners to glance in their direction. With tears falling she stated with complete finality, "I don't want to 'ear any more of your lies, Brody. Maybe. And I'm not sure about this. But maybe somewhere in there," she indicated his body, top to toe, "is a good person trying to get out. But you are a manipulating cheat and a compulsive liar, Brody Taylor. You 'ave the morals of an alley cat. I 'ave never been so betrayed."

Mel turned and bolted out of the restaurant.

Numbly, Brody watched her leave, knowing all was lost. Through the window, he watched her hail a cab and jump in. She never looked back.

He finished the sentence he had started, "— love you." It came out as a choked whisper.

Brody lowered his eyes, suddenly conscious of the waiting staff and other diners staring at him.

His gaze fell on the USB stick with all its incriminating evidence against HTL. Mel hadn't taken it. Absently, he wondered what to do with it. He had no axe to grind against HTL. The whole pentest had been a means to an end for him, not that it had worked out the way he had hoped. When he'd taken on the assignment he'd signed a non-disclosure agreement. One that up until a few minutes ago he'd been prepared to completely violate in order to win over Mel. But, now that she had made her decision, he might as well destroy the USB stick and, at the very least, maintain some level of professional integrity.

Surely that was something?

He called the waiter over and paid the bill. The other diners returned to their meals and conversations.

But Brody didn't care what happened to HTL. And what the hell was a he — a social engineer who manipulated almost everyone he met — doing caring about professional integrity.

He stood up, leaving the incriminating USB stick lying on the table.

Fate would decide.

Brody sunk his hands deep in his pockets and, with hunched shoulders, walked out of the restaurant.

THE END

ACKNOWLEDGEMENTS

Thank you for reading *Social Engineer*, which is a standalone prequel to *Invasion of Privacy*. My objective was to introduce the world to Brody Taylor, the elite hacker protagonist of Invasion of Privacy, in a short, accessible, standalone adventure. It's often hard for readers invest their time and money and take a chance on an unknown debut author and so I hope that this short novella has intrigued you enough to want to take that chance now, by choosing to read Invasion of Privacy. And its future sequels.

There is a team of people around me who I'd like to thank. First there is my editor, Bryony Sutherland (no relation!) for improving the manuscript immensely and Peter O'Connor of bespokebookcovers.com who designed the fantastic cover. Then there's my wife, Cheryl, and daughters, Laura and Raquel, who fill my life completely, (and also double up fantastic proof readers). Thank you all.

Now read the beginning of Invasion of Privacy by Ian Sutherland, the first full-length novel featuring Brody Taylor.

Invasion of Privacy

A brutal killing takes place in an office meeting room in London. The victim is a beautiful young cellist, lured to a fake audition for the Royal Opera House orchestra.

MURDERS: Detective Inspector Jenny Price investigates, baffled by how the killer knew so much about the victim.

WEBCAMS: Does the answer lie in a website that broadcasts webcam feeds from inside homes, offices and shops? Expert security consultant Brody Taylor, hired to test the highly secure site's cyber-defences by its anonymous owner, begins to suspect so.

VOYEURS: As the residents of thousands of households across the country carry on their day-to-day lives, oblivious to the fact that are being observed at all times by the site's paying customers, one very sadistic voyeur selects his next target, a sultry Swedish *au pair*.

Thrown together, can Brody and Jenny find a way to bring down the site and track down the serial killer before it's too late? But can Jenny trust the charming but mysterious security consultant?

CHAPTER 1

Anna Parker wished she'd paid attention to the doubts buried deep in her mind. That they'd put two fingers in each cheek and whistled. Cried foul. Screamed. Anything to have made her listen to sense. To have helped her see through the charade. For she now knew that's all it was — an elaborate sham that had lured her to this abrupt ending.

"What will you play?" the man named William Webber had asked ten minutes before, when the three-day old illusion was still in full swing and Anna was completely oblivious.

"Elgar's *Concerto in E-Minor*," she replied. Her voice cracked as she spoke, her nervousness sneaking past her lips, betraying the confident image she hoped to portray. She inhaled deeply, knowing from other auditions that this would help calm her nerves.

"Please begin when you are ready," Webber said.

She sat on a lonely chair in the centre of the meeting room, her cello propped on its endpin, the neck resting reassuringly on her shoulder. Anna looked around. Desks lined the edges in a large horseshoe shape. Webber sat cross-legged at the head of the room, in front of an imposing wall-to-wall whiteboard. Overhead a huge projector was suspended from the ceiling. In one corner a sprawling fake plastic plant bestowed upon the insipid space a pretence of life. Anna glanced through the window that spanned the length of one wall. In the distance, she could just see the London Eye slowly rotating, each glass pod packed full of tourists.

Bravely, she gave voice to her concerns. "This is an odd place to hold an audition?"

His eyes flashed briefly. Annoyance perhaps? But then he fingered his beard, offering an air of contemplation.

"Yes, I suppose it is," he smiled tightly. "But the acoustics are good enough for our purposes. Please begin."

Anna wasn't sure she concurred. A meeting room in an office building wasn't exactly designed for musical recitals. But the environment was only half of what had been bothering her.

"From your email, I thought someone from the ROH would be here?"

Webber paused, considering her question.

The email inviting Anna to audition for a place in the Orchestra of the Royal Opera House had arrived in her inbox three days ago. It explained that she had been selected for audition on the recommendation of Jake Symmonds, one of the viola professors at Trinity Laban Conservatoire of Music and Dance, where she studied cello. Although Anna wasn't taught by Jake she knew who he was. She briefly considered that perhaps the email was a prank by one of her four student housemates, all of whom knew it was her dream to play professionally. She dismissed this thought — surely her friends wouldn't be so cruel. No, it was just a straightforward email with a potentially life-changing offer.

Anna's flattered ego soon took over, suppressing her doubts. Of course it was standard practice, she reasoned, for the Royal Opera House Orchestra to consult one of London's leading musical conservatoires as to which of its students to audition. Of course it was normal, she convinced herself, for a viola professor she'd never met to know of her virtuosity as a cellist. Teachers discussed their students with each other all the time, didn't they? Of course it was fair — no, more than that — it was *fitting* for Anna to be given the chance to fulfil her lifelong dream of playing in a professional orchestra years ahead of her peers.

After a few minutes of consternation — or maybe it had been only a few seconds — she embraced the email for what it was: an official invitation to audition for one of the most prestigious orchestras in the country. She felt the excitement build in her and, like a dam made of matchsticks, it quickly burst. With tears cascading happily down her cheeks she jumped up and down on her mattress, screaming for joy, just as she had done one Christmas Day morning years before, when Santa had left an exquisitely laminated maple cello at the foot of her bed.

"As I said to you in the lift on the way up, Miss Parker," Webber responded, "I'm simply the first round. An initial screening, so to speak."

"But —"

"Put it this way. Impress me today, and next Tuesday you'll be in the ROH at Covent Garden for the final stage of the audition."

Anna paused for a moment and allowed his words to sink in. She imagined herself in the orchestra pit, tuned and ready for the conductor to lift his baton, the ballet dancers waiting in the wings, the audience hushing, and finally, the curtains opening. It was a delicious image and she desperately wanted it to happen. To happen to her: the cellist who had evolved from that little girl with the best ever Christmas present. The girl who had worked so hard, first learning the basics — bowing, rhythm, and reading notes — and, in time, attempting to recreate euphonic perfection. Countless hours of solitary practice. Daily sacrifices. A childhood spent observing her school friends through the living room window playing forty-forty, kerbie and later, kiss-chase, while she practised her scales over and over, her bow movements across the strings becoming autonomic as muscle memory took over, the melodies becoming more complex and harmonious.

Anna forced a smile onto her face. "Okay then. I'll do my best."

He nodded. "Whenever you're ready, Anna."

She took two more deep breaths, drew back the bow and launched into the concerto, her favourite piece. The music, as Elgar had planned, came slowly and hauntingly at first. Within a few bars she was lost to the stately rhythm of her part. Webber disappeared from her thoughts, even though she could see him immediately opposite her. It was as if someone else was observing him through her eyes, so lost was she in the music.

Webber began to wave his arms as if conducting her. Although his timing was slightly out, he became quite animated, his eyes closing in rapture.

Anna, too, closed her eyes and within a few bars, had completely surrendered herself to the magnificent piece. She felt as though she was achieving a level of grace that she knew was denied her in any other aspect of her life. The bow in her right hand elegantly flew left and right over the strings. Her left hand moved up and down the fingerboard, rapidly depressing the strings, the positions fluent and clear, each note perfect.

She reached the final crescendo with a flourish. She knew that she had never played better and that Tuesday would see her in Covent Garden. A bead of sweat trickled down her back. She opened her eyes, smiling expectantly.

Webber was nowhere to be seen.

She swivelled on the chair, scanning the room in panic. He was right behind her, one arm raised high, holding what looked like a large dagger, a maniacal grin spread across his face.

Uncomprehending, she asked, "What are you . . ."

Webber rapidly swung his arm downwards, twisting his wrist at the last second to cause the solid base of the dagger's handle to strike Anna cruelly across the side of her face. Her head exploded in pain, whiteness obscuring her vision. She dropped to the floor. Her cello and bow fell from her hands, clattering on top of her, numbed notes emitting from the instrument's strings as it fell to the floor beside her. Alongside the pain Anna instantly became nauseous, as if she'd downed too much tequila too quickly. Tears streamed from her eyes, mingling with the blood oozing from a gash on her cheek. She covered her head with her hands and crunched into a foetal position.

The image of Dorothy from *The Wizard of Oz*, her favourite movie as a child, flickered into her mind. She saw Dorothy holding back the curtain, exposing the charlatan behind the illusion, and accusing him of being *a very bad man*.

Anna forced her heavy lids to open. Her own version of a *very bad man* was leaning down towards her, the point of his gleaming dagger held out in front of him, the illusion he had held her in for three days now completely shattered. She glimpsed past the sharp point and into Webber's eyes — black, lustful and full of malicious intent — and saw her death in them.

Fathoming that she had just given her final performance, yet oddly grateful to have played so perfectly, Anna felt her eyelids droop again as she allowed herself to drift towards welcome blackness.

CHAPTER 2

"I'm here for a 9:00 a.m. interview with Richard Wilkie. My name is Brody Taylor."

The pudgy receptionist pushed her glasses further up the bridge of her nose and checked her computer screen. She squinted in confusion.

"We don't have a Mr Wilkie based in this office."

"Yes, sorry. It's a video interview. He's calling in from Dubai."

"Ah, I see. Yes, here you are. The ground floor video conferencing suite is booked for you, Mr Taylor."

The receptionist printed off a security pass, pressed a button to open the gate, allowed him to pass through and escorted him to a meeting room labelled 'VC1'. She pushed open the door and allowed him to enter.

Impressive. She was efficient and security conscious. It made a pleasant change.

"When Mr Wilkie dials in, it should answer automatically. Is there anything I can get you? Tea, coffee perhaps?"

"I'm fine, thanks." Brody gave his best sheepish smile. "Maybe you could just wish me luck?"

She smiled obligingly. "Good luck, Mr Taylor." She shut the door behind her.

Brody quickly surveyed the room. An oval board table took up the length of the room, but looked like it had been cut in half lengthways, with six black leather seats on the curved side facing onto a massive elongated video screen, actually made up of three widescreen monitors placed side-by-side. Above the centre screen was a unit housing three cameras angled to capture two seats each. Brody knew from experience that when the Cisco TelePresence system activated, the screens would display a similarly furnished room located somewhere else in the world, giving both parties the optical illusion of one complete boardroom.

Brody dropped his leather laptop case on the table and rummaged around inside. He removed his tablet computer and placed it in front of him, flipping it open to reveal its detachable keyboard. He then pulled out a roll of silver duct tape and peeled off three strips, sticking them over the cameras. Grinning to himself at the irony of employing such a low-tech solution, he pushed a panel set into the board table and revealed the touchscreen tablet that controlled the TelePresence system. Deftly he muted the microphones in the room he was in and then searched through the address book. Twenty other Atlas Brands Inc. video conferencing suites were listed by city name. Brody chose Dubai and pressed the green button.

The screens jumped to life. Suddenly, an image of six other people sat opposite him, chit-chatting with each other. The older man in the centre noticed that someone had dialled in. His brows furrowed. "Who's that dialling in from Birmingham? Is there something wrong with your video system? It's just a black screen here."

Brody used the touchscreen control panel to send a text message to their system in Dubai. *Yes, it's Rich Wilkie here. I can see and hear you guys fine. Must be a glitch. Don't worry, I'll message you like this if I've got anything to say.*

Brody watched the older man read his message displayed on their screen three thousand miles away.

"Okay Rich. No problem. How's the weather in the UK?"

Brody typed out his answer. *It's raining, Andrew. It's April. Would you expect anything else?*

Andrew Lamont, Chief Executive Officer of Atlas Brands Inc., laughed. The woman on his left said, "Look, here's Chu in Sydney."

At that moment, the image in Brody's room shrunk to just the middle monitor, destroying the illusion of them all being in the same room. The right hand monitor suddenly displayed another room, with just one inhabitant. It was labelled Sydney. A few moments later, the remaining left-hand screen was taken up by Munich, with three people.

Spread across the globe, the board of directors of the world's fourth largest restaurant chain and hospitality company greeted each other amiably.

"Okay, it looks as though we're all here," said Lamont. "Let's get this meeting started. For you folks in Sydney and Munich wondering about the black screen, that's Rich Wilkie in Birmingham. Seems to be a problem with the system there, but he can hear us all fine. Right, let's get down to business. Ulf, can you take us through the agenda?"

Ulf Lubber, the middle of the three people in the Munich

office, walked everyone through the agenda. The item Brody was here for was fourth on the agenda, at least an hour away. He zoned out of the meeting and connected his tablet computer to the Internet via its built-in 4G SIM card. He might as well use the time productively.

Brody worked his way through his emails, spread across numerous accounts, most of which were newsletters and blog posts from the various technology and computer hacking websites he subscribed to anonymously.

While he worked, he kept one eye and one ear on the meeting. Heather Bell, Atlas Brand's Chief Financial Officer, presented the prior month's financial performance of each of their major restaurant chains, all famous brands in their local regions. Walter Chan, who managed the property portfolio, took them through expansion plans by country. Heng Chu, the Chief Information Officer sitting on his own in the Sydney office, struggled his way through his plans to integrate the IT systems of four recent restaurant chain acquisitions Atlas had made in Asia, frequently interrupted when it became clear the synergy savings the board had promised the shareholders would take much longer to realise.

"What's next, Ulf?" asked Lamont.

"We've got Marketing and the launch plans for a brand new concept." Ulf turned to the man on his right in Munich. "Over to you Tim."

Brody looked up from his computer and focused on the meeting. Adrenalin began to pump through his bloodstream.

Tim Welland, Chief Marketing Officer, began his presentation. He had connected his laptop to the TelePresence system and its screen took over the central monitor, forcing the images of the other meeting rooms to tile next to each other, now even smaller. Welland took them through a polished PowerPoint presentation, illustrated by concept artwork.

"Welcome to Barbecue Union, a brand new mid-range dining concept for the UK, Canada and Germany. Every table in our Barbecue Union outlets will have a live barbecue grille embedded within it, which customers will use to cook their own food. The food will be presented on skewers along with a selection of marinades. It will be a mix of Mediterranean, Indian, Oriental, and American cuisine. Imagine, if you will, all the fun of having your food cooked in front of you, just like the Japanese Teppanyaki restaurants, but without the expensively trained chefs. Yes, you guessed it, our customers will be those chefs."

Welland paused and surveyed his colleagues on the screens. Lots of nodding heads.

He continued his presentation, dropping into lower levels of detail, eventually hitting target market demographics, pricing strategies, menus, and launch costs. "And the best bit is that much of the marketing will be word-of-mouth; the best kind. As customers experience this totally new concept, they will mention it to everyone they know."

With a touch of triumph, Welland concluded his presentation and began taking questions. While they debated the pros and cons of this new chain, Brody pressed a button on the control tablet and the image of his room was added to the others. Just a black screen. He stood up and peeled the duct tape from the webcams in his room, revealing his face in close up on the screen, his swept back white blond hair, green eyes and carefully groomed beard filling the screen. He sat back down, his every move mirrored on the screen, and unmuting his microphone, waited for someone to notice.

"What about hygiene? Surely we'd be liable to local food safety regulations if the customers don't cook the ingredients properly?"

asked Annabel Fielding, their Head of Legal, located in the Dubai office.

Just as Welland began to answer, Ulf Lubber in Germany exclaimed, "Who's that?" He pointed at his screen, the others following his direction.

Brody waved and said, "Hi."

On his tablet, Brody absent-mindedly noticed a new email arrive. He automatically clicked it open.

"Who the hell are you, young man?" demanded Andrew Lamont. "And where's Rich Wilkie?"

"Me?" said Brody innocently, forcing himself to ignore the email. It could wait.

"I know who it is," said Chu in Sydney. "He's a 'white hat' security consultant called Brody Taylor. I recently contracted him to carry out a pentest. But what he's doing there I've no idea!"

"What the hell is a pentest?" asked the CEO.

Brody stepped in. "A penetration test is a simulated attack on your organisation's security defences to identify weaknesses. It's done through computer hacking or social engineering or, as I've done, with a combination of both."

"Social engineering?" prompted Lamont.

"The art of manipulating people into performing actions or divulging confidential information to give me the access I need. And, as you can clearly see, I've successfully broken through your security defences and have been sitting in on your board meeting for the last hour. But fortunately for you, the last part of a pentest is to report back the findings. And that's what I'm here to do."

Lamont turned on the CIO. "Did you agree to this, Chu?"

In Sydney, Chu visibly squirmed in his chair. "No. Mr Taylor was supposed to meet with me next week to present his findings.

From there, I would block any holes he found and make sure we're completely secure from a real cyber attack."

Lamont turned back to Brody. "Okay, Mr Taylor, you've proved your point. Thank you for what you've done. Why don't you leave us to our board meeting and report back to Chu as planned."

"Hold on a second," said Fielding. "Did you get him to sign a confidentiality agreement, Chu? He's just heard all about our recent performance and future plans!"

"Yes, of course I did," said Chu.

Brody nodded in agreement. Rising from his seat, he paused halfway and asked. "Before I go, do you mind if I ask you one question, Mr Chu?"

Lamont splayed his hands in exasperation and shook his head in disbelief.

"Why did you hire me for a pentest right now?"

"What do you mean?" asked Chu.

"Why now? Why not a year ago? Or in three months from now?"

"It's part of our security improvement programme. We do this kind of thing all the time in IT."

"From the vulnerabilities I've exposed, I very much doubt that, Mr Chu." Brody looked at Lamont. "Mr Lamont, why don't you ask Mr Chu the same question? Maybe you'll get a straight answer."

Lamont's intent expression showed that he knew there was more going on here than was immediately apparent. "Chu?"

Chu shrugged. "I was talking with Welland about the plans for launching the new restaurant concept. He was worried that one of our competitors might break in and steal our ideas. As I've explained previously, IT doesn't have anywhere near the budget necessary to put in place a comprehensive threat protection programme. So Welland offered to pay for a pentest to at least determine how exposed we are. Who am I to turn down a gift horse like that?"

"That makes sense, doesn't it?" asked Brody. "No more to it."

Tim Welland, the man who'd waxed lyrical about his new restaurant concept a few minutes before, was strangely silent. He clasped his hands together.

"Welland, what's going on?"

"It's as Chu said."

"It's called corporate espionage, Mr Lamont." Brody said, sitting back down. "And your company is guilty of it right now. The last time I heard about a case like this was in the hotel industry. Hilton settled out of court with Starwood for $85 million."

Lamont blew his top, spittle flying everywhere. "What the fuck is going on here?"

All the executives silently studied their hands.

"The funny thing about the presentation you've just heard from Mr Welland is that I've already read about an exceptionally similar concept for a grille-based barbecue restaurant chain. But in the documents I read there was one significant difference. Your number one competitor's logo was all over them. Would you like to know where I found these documents, Mr Lamont?"

"Go on . . ." said Lamont tightly.

"As I've already mentioned, your security defences are so weak I was able to give myself access to each of your email accounts and —"

"You've read our private email?" shrieked Fielding.

"Well, yes. Fascinating reading. But the most interesting were the documents I found in Mr Welland's account."

"I can explain . . ." pleaded Welland.

As Welland attempted to defend himself under constant barrage from his CEO, Head of Legal and most of the other board members, Brody zoned out and read the email that had popped into his inbox earlier. It was from one of the members of CrackerHack entitled, *Favour Required - Will Reciprocate.* CrackerHack was an online forum used by computer hackers from all over the world to brag about their exploits and swap ideas, tips and techniques. Brody spent much of his spare time on there. The message was from a member called Crooner42, a username that Brody vaguely recognised from some of the discussion threads. Crooner42 had blasted it out to all of the subscribers to a forum entitled 'Advanced Pentest Techniques'. In it, Crooner42 explained that he had built an experimental live video-feed based Internet site that was likely to attract unwarranted attention from law agencies around the world. He'd hardened it as best he could, but needed someone deeply skilled to pentest it thoroughly, to ensure it couldn't be broken into or brought down.

Brody wondered what the 'experimental' site was for.

Crooner42 requested that members of the forum declare their interest in carrying out the work. He would then choose from one of the respondents. Brody expected that Crooner42 would select someone based on reviewing his historical activity on the site. Brody knew he would be a strong candidate and, with the Atlas Brands job now pretty much finished, was sorely tempted to offer his services. In return, Crooner42 was bartering a week's worth of his own coding services. That could always come in handy. It wasn't a bad trade for what would probably amount to just a few hours of work.

"Do you have proof of this allegation, Mr Taylor?"

Brody looked up. Lamont had asked the question.

"Well, yes of course. Give me a second."

Brody opened a new browser tab and brought up an email he had drafted earlier. He pressed send.

"I've just forwarded you all some emails sent to Mr Welland from a Janis Taplow. I believe she's a relatively new employee within the marketing organisation. Where did you hire Janis from, Tim?"

Tim Welland replied flatly. He named their number one competitor.

"The email contains the whole launch campaign for their grille restaurant concept, presentations, financial plans, target countries, demographics, everything. And, if you open up the main presentation, you'll notice that even the concept art is very similar. In fact, the only main difference is the name of the restaurant chain."

"Got it," said Lubber, Chu and Fielding in concert, from three different locations around the world.

As they read through the offending material, Brody flipped back to Crooner42's request. He was tempted by the job, but hesitant to put himself forward until he reviewed the site in question. It was the reference to it receiving unwarranted attention from law agencies that intrigued him.

Incredulity rang in the voices from the screen as they absorbed the material Brody had just emailed them.

He checked Crooner42's profile. He presented himself as more of a coder than a hacker, someone who spent far more time programming than trying to identify exploits in systems. He'd been active on CrackerHack for three years. Satisfied, Brody clicked on the hyperlink to the so-called 'experimental' site. It was called www.SecretlyWatchingYou.com. It seemed to be a random collection of network camera and webcam feeds. Brody clicked on one, making sure his computer's speakers were muted. It showed some people working in an office, layers of desks and desktop computers. Another feed showed some fish swimming around in a fish tank. Not particularly interesting.

The Internet was full of webcam sites, the majority of which were either for viewing public places from afar in real time or for pornographic purposes. But this site claimed to have hacked into private network cameras in peoples' homes and workplaces. It was certainly unusual. It charged fees for access beyond the free taster webcam feeds on the front page. Brody couldn't really see why anyone would want to pay or what all the fuss about law agencies was about.

Surely Crooner42 was over-egging the protection the site needed to have? Who would bother to attack it? And publicly requesting help like this on CrackerHack was definitely out of the ordinary. But then Brody remembered that after this meeting, his diary was looking concerningly clear. If Crooner42 selected Brody over other forum members for the job, his elite status in the hacking community would intensify — doubly so if he quickly broke through the website's security countermeasures.

Ah, what the hell!

He returned to the original email and pressed the link Crooner42 had provided. In the blink of an eye, he had registered his interest in carrying out the pentest on SecretlyWatchingYou. Now it was down to whether Crooner42 chose him over another offer.

Brody returned his attention to the video conference.

"Looks like I'm done here," said Tim Welland, getting to his feet in Munich.

"That's the understatement of the day," commented Chu.

"You'll have my resignation in your inbox within the hour, Mr Lamont." They all waited while Welland gathered his belongings and left the room in Germany.

"Well, Mr Taylor," said Lamont. "A bit unorthodox, but I'd like to thank you for saving our company from a very embarrassing predicament, not to mention the potential law suits."

"Just doing my job."

"I think we should delay the presentation of your findings report until I'm back in the UK, which will be Monday week. I'd also like to personally shake your hand. And if everything is as insecure as you describe, it looks as though Chu will see a lot more budget going his way."

"Sounds good to me," said Brody.

"And me," said Chu, his relief evident.

Ten minutes later, Brody drove out of the Atlas Brands car park in his metallic orange and black, custom-designed Smart Fortwo coupe. It would take a good few hours to get back to London. His phone vibrated. He slowed, looked down and glanced at the message header. It was from Crooner42 and entitled 'Pentest Outcome . . .'

Brody stopped the car and clicked on the message, fully expecting to see his name in lights.

He couldn't believe what he read.

ABOUT IAN SUTHERLAND

Ian Sutherland was brought up the Outer Hebrides, idyllic remote islands off the west coast of Scotland. In an effort to escape the monotonous miles of heather, bracken and wild sheep, Ian read avidly, dreaming of one day arriving in a big city like London. And then, at the tender age of 12 he was unexpectedly uprooted to Peckham, an inner city suburb of South-East London. Ian quickly discovered that the real London was a damn sight more gritty and violent than the version in his books and shown on tv. Undeterred, Ian did what he did best, and buried his head in books, dreaming of other places to escape to.

Roll forward some years and Ian can still be found with his head in a book. Or, given that he enjoyed a successful career in the IT industry, an eBook Reader. And now, having travelled a fair bit of the globe in person and even more of it via the Internet, Ian lives with his wife and two daughters in a small idyllic village, surrounded by green fields, copses and the occasional sheep, yet located just outside of the London he finally came to love.

Here, he writes gritty, violent crime thrillers full of well-rounded characters, set in and around non-touristy London. His stories also feature the online world that most of us jump into blindly each day, but Ian exposes its underbelly and dramatically illustrates how dangerous the internet can be for the unwary.

Learn more about Ian at www.ianhsutherland.com
Join his mailing list at www.ianhsutherland.com/stay-in-touch

Follow him on twitter at www.twitter.com/iansuth
Like his Facebook page at www.facebook.com/ihsutherland

Printed in Great Britain
by Amazon